FOG A DOX

BRUCE PASCOE

Magabala Books

First published by Magabala Books Aboriginal Corporation, Broome, Western
Australia in 2012 Website: www.magabala.com Email: sales@magabala.com

Magabala Books receives financial assistance from the Commonwealth
Government through the Australia Council, its arts advisory body. The State
of Western Australia has made an investment in this project through the
Department of Culture and the Arts in association with Lotterywest.

Designed by Tracey Gibbs
Illustrations by Brenda Marshall
Printed in China at Everbest Printing Company

Cataloguing-in-Publication available from the National Library of Australia
ISBN 978-1-921248-55-9

Australian Government

Australia Council
for the Arts

Government of Western Australia
Department of Culture and the Arts

lotterywest

FOR BRIM, A DINGO DOG

LYREBIRDS

Albert Cutts was a tree feller. A fella who cuts down trees.

People will always need wood for their houses, he told the possums, but the possums always needed apples for their mouths and only ever really concentrated when food was involved. In any case they *lived* in trees and couldn't see the sense in cutting them down. So they just glared at Albert even though the apples were off his tree.

Albert didn't cut down trees for nothing — that

was his job. No-one knew the bush as well or loved it more deeply. He lived in a hut beside a stream deep in the forest. He built the hut with planks split from forest timber, the roof from bark peeled off logs.

Albert was happy there. The only time he got really annoyed was when he heard his kettle whistling its head off when he was way up in the hills cutting logs.

'I didn't leave the kettle on,' he muttered to himself, 'I'm sure I didn't.' He put his axe down, covered his lunch box with a piece of bark to keep the magpies and currawongs away, and walked down the hill, plodded across the creek flat, and stepped from stone to stone to cross the stream, the kettle whistling madly all the while, fit to burn itself out and he couldn't afford that, he only had one kettle and he'd seen the price of new ones. Oh, he loved his cups of tea.

He stepped through the door and stared at the wood stove. No kettle. It was where he left it, safely on the brick beside the sink.

'Lyrebird, that bloomin' lyrebird again,' he said to the owl that liked to roost on the rafter beside the chimney. Nice and warm up there, and the only inconvenience was having to wait for Albert to let him out at night. But Albert was as reliable as the sun in that regard.

The owl blinked at the unusual anger in Albert's voice and said nothing, not a hoot, but then you never got much in the way of conversation from owls. Besides, the owl knew the tricks a lyrebird could play, had been fooled itself by the bird imitating squeaking bush mice and rabbits.

'That's the third time he's got me,' growled Albert, 'third time I've left work to come back to the hut, about time I woke up to it.' But what if it really was the kettle? He couldn't afford to let it burn out.

'Bloomin' lyrebird makin' me miss all that work.' Never mind, he thought, it gives me a chance to stoke the fire and check on Brim.

Albert's dog Brim was slumped in the corner on an old wheat bag as five voracious pups sucked at her teats, mewling in their anxiety to get as much milk as they could, pushing at her with insistent little paws and butting her with their greedy muzzles.

Brim followed Albert's movements, a wistful, yearning expression in her eyes. She missed being up on the ridge tops with the old bloke, sometimes snooping about the fox and wallaby trails, sometimes sleeping in the sun, dreaming of having a good chase through the trees. And sometimes she just did what dogs are very good at: scratching. Nothing like a good scratch, followed by a little sniff of the air, a glance at Albert, and then a little dog-think, which never took very long because, well, dogs never think for long; food always looms too large in their mind and blots out anything but the thought of a bone buried near the woodheap — or was it under the verandah, or the apple tree? Oh, well, I forget where, I'll have to check them all.

Albert would sometimes catch Brim as one of her thoughts evaporated under the dominant influence of bone memories and call out to her, 'Lose concentration again, darlin'? It happens my furry princess, even to the best brains. One minute we're working out how many eight-bee-one planks in a sixty-foot log and next minute we're thinkin' of rabbit stew. It happens, ol' darlin', and that's a fact.'

But what Albert didn't know was that Brim had been teaching herself to count. Don't laugh, dogs can count. Smart dogs, anyway.

For instance the bone under the verandah, or apple tree, or woodheap or … anyway, that bone is one bone. One. And the rabbit that ran under the dunny. One rabbit. One. She knew it was one because if there'd been two, *two*, she wouldn't know which one to chase. Simple, counting.

And foxes. Like last winter when she had seen a pack of them sitting in silhouette on the ridgeline staring down at their chookhouse. Brim counted them. One fox, two fox, ah, ah, where'd I leave that bone? I hope them fox don't get it, now, where was I? Oh yes, one fox, two fox, ah, ah, lotsa foxes. See, I *can* count past two.

But no counting foxes today. Too busy with the pups, look at them all, one pup, two pups, gee their little claws scratch … ah, one pup, two pups, ah, ah, piles of pups. There, did it again, counting.

'How are the pups goin', Brim? Got 'em under control, have ya?' Albert knelt down and stroked his dog's head. She flattened her ears and stuck out the tip of her pink tongue. Gees she loved that Albert.

'You're a good dog, Brim, a real good dog.' He rubbed her between the ears and around the back of her neck and she closed her eyes in delight. Gees she loved that Albert.

He stroked the silky muzzles of the pups, two of them asleep with Brim's teats in their mouths. 'Gees you're good little pups,' he murmured as he inspected their delicate pink paws, so innocent, so new, never walked on rough ground, never chased a cat, never felt pain. 'Beautiful little boorais,' the old man murmured, unconsciously using the Maap word for babies.

His grandfather taught him that. Old Grandad Shorty. Short Cutts, get it, very funny. Grandad Shorty only knew a dozen or so words of his mother's Maap language but that was better than nothing.

Old Shorty was pretty dark, but most blokes who worked in the forest splitting railway sleepers were like that. Wood sap, charcoal, sweat, they got in your pores. And Albert was much the same. Years of cutting trees had stained the creases in his hands, years of grubbing out roots, splitting posts, burning off the heads, well, you got a bit brown, so no-one remarked too much about Albert's colour, he was much like any other old bloke in the bush.

Albert's secret was that he not only knew some words of the old language, but he used them too. Mirrigan for dog, buln buln for lyrebird, wagra for crow, goomera the old possum, googai the owl beside the chimney, they all knew the sound of their own names, got used to Albert addressing them with respect.

That's how Brim got her name. Old Grandad Shorty told a story about his own grandmother Daisy being born under a tree on the bank of Lake Brim. Old Shorty remembered Granny Daisy bringing him up on a diet of condensed milk, bread and Golden Syrup ... and stories, bush stories: why the red gums grow where they grow, why the magpie is black and white, and a bit of a rude one about why dogs sniff each other's bums. One day all the dogs went to a big fancy dress ball and they left their tails ...

'Ah, I'd better get back to work,' Albert told

Brim, 'but I'm glad to see you've got your own tail, my old darlin'.'

Albert stumped his way up the hill where his axe and wedges waited on a day's hard labour. The hills and valleys soon chimed to the strokes of his axe and the ring of the mallet on the steel wedge as he split posts. It was hard work, but pleasant enough, with the company of a yellow robin perched slantwise on a trunk, watching with eyes like little black pearls, sharp to any grubs or larvae exposed by Albert's work.

The kookaburra, kuark, was usually there too, a beak like a pair of tin snips kept sharp for any lizard or snake silly enough to come out in the open. Currawongs and magpies stood by with a show of disdain for human endeavour but their greedy beaks never refused the big white wood grubs that Albert dislodged from their tunnels in the logs.

For Albert it was like being surrounded by friends and relations, some of them close and confidential, others haughty and a bit superior, some frantic to fill their bellies or, like the grey thrush, harried to exhaustion by a coronet of gaping beaks squalling their hunger.

Even the goanna would sidle up from time to time, sometimes saggy and baggy in dull grey flaking skin, but after he'd rubbed that off against the coarse bark of a messmate he appeared bright yellow and black, like an enamelled prince.

Albert loved the bush. Some would say it was a lonely life, eating a solitary lunch on a rocky hillside surrounded by the debris of fallen logs and split posts, but most times Albert had Brim to talk to and on the rare occasions when she couldn't, like when she was suckling pups, there were the animals; bird song glinting from the tree tops, butterflies winking at him with the opening and shutting of brand new wings still damp from the cocoon.

Albert rested against a stump he'd cut in … now, when was it? Before Brim was born, yes, even before her mother, old Kudja, about a year or two before the last big flood, so it'd have to be, yes, 1972 or thereabouts, a long time anyway. The tree he felled today would be that tree's sister, and thirty metres away there was a tree that he might cut in another twenty years … Well, maybe. Maybe he'd still be swinging an axe in twenty years, or a chainsaw if he ever lowered himself to use a chainsaw, or could afford to buy one. Eight hundred and eighty dollars they were, and that's 160 posts or two week's work, nah, stick to the axe, Albert, cuts all right … and quieter too.

Brim would be coming with him again in a few days because the pups were getting bigger and she'd be wanting a rest from them soon, the little devils. Their father was one of the bush dingoes, as Brim's own father had been. The dog that mated with Brim was nearly pure dingo, dark like the mountain dingoes are, a kind of golden chocolate with swatches of near-black at the nape and flanks. He was a beautiful dog, sharp as a tack. He'd quiz you with his eyes, trying to learn about you: if he could trust you, whether you were the kind of bloke who shot creatures out of arrogance, just because he could, just because he had the power of death within the reach of his finger.

They'd only caught each other's eye a few times,

but each time it felt to Albert like an interrogation. What sort of man are you? How do you treat your dogs? Do you keep your chooks locked up at night? Would you get cranky if I fell in love with Brim or are you prejudiced against dingoes? That sort of look. They respected each other but they'd never be mates, a wild animal and a man, never mates, deferential acquaintances, but never mates, because when a dog became the mate of a man he lost his wildness, lost the freedom to decide where he slept at night and the right to grab rabbits by the back of the neck.

With his hat tipped over his eyes and his mug of tea cooling beside him Albert damn near dozed off before he roused himself from contemplation of the canine universe and let his hand fall on the smooth, hard shank of his axe, his uncomplaining work companion of thirty-five years ... Well, it'd had nine or so handles and this was the third head, but it was still the same axe.

He rose, his knees creaking, and slowly arched his back, stretching the tired muscles of his shoulders before striding over to the fallen log and belting the wedge into a radial crack, driving it deeper and deeper until the post sprang out of the log like a miracle.

'Good splittin' wood this stringybark,' Albert mused for the thousandth time, then fell silent as a strange whining, piping cry reached his ear. He twisted and turned about to fix the position of the cry, wondering if it was the little communal mew that currawongs peeped to each other as they searched for food, or the choughs who liked to march about together like a band of scarlet-eyed horticulturalists, turning over the forest litter, and remarking convivially on the fascination of moss and liverworts, mushroom mycelium and scrub worms.

But if it was choughs they'd eventually march into the clearing in their neat parade and if it was currawongs you'd never mistake their gangsta rap. No, it was an animal. He listened again …
A baby animal.

He leant the mallet against the log and walked quietly toward the noise, careful to avoid standing on twigs that might snap or dry eucalypt leaves that might betray him with their crunch. He stood still and waited, sure he was close to the source of the noise. A group of granite boulders stood only twenty metres from him and he moved forward and to his right so that he might see around them. He met the fierce eyes of a goshawk, defiant, challenging.

The bird at first lowered its head in a show of aggression but when Albert stood his ground, trying to see what the goshawk gripped in its talons the raptor stood to its full height, puffing out the hackles on its neck and chest and lifting its wings, trying to produce the illusion of having doubled in size. Despite the mad yellow glare of its truculent eyes, Albert refused to be intimidated.

He leaned closer and could see at last what the bird protected so zealously: a baby fox, a tiny carcass from which the simitar beak had already torn strips of flesh. Albert scanned the area and saw the hole dug beneath the granite tor and the flattened area before it where the baby foxes had been playing, for yes, there were surely others in the den and they must have become impatient waiting for their mother and ventured out to play in the sun.

Why hadn't the mother returned? She would have heard the goshawk's attack call. Had the mother taken a bait, been shot by bounty hunters, killed by an angry farmer who'd stayed up all night to see what had been raiding his chookpen? Albert backed away. There was nothing he could do for the little fox. The goshawk was probably desperate to feed its own young. Killing rabbits and mice was what goshawks did for a living but if a baby fox got too bold while its mother was away they'd swoop on that too. That's how the world goes around, rabbits eat the hearts out of Mrs Maloney's wattle seedlings and goshawks eat the rabbits *and* Mrs Maloney's chickens if she's out for the day, drinking strong black tea on another lady's front verandah. 'Aren't the foxes bad this year, Mrs Maloney.' 'And the hawks, Mrs Bortolotto, there's one been keeping a wicked yellow eye on my chickens. Give it a good whack with the broom if I catch him.'

But Mrs Maloney's chickens are safe for another

day because the goshawk's nestlings will feed on baby fox meat tonight.

Albert split out his quota of posts but before it got dark he returned to the granite boulders and inspected the beaten sand at the entrance to the den. No adult fox had snuck back to the cubs while he had been working. They were orphans.

He knelt at the entrance and the acrid fox scent was overwhelming. He reached his arm in and followed the tunnel as it curved sharply beneath the granite. He could just feel the fur of an animal … and its teeth. The brave little fellow was trying to bite his hand. He clasped the tiny body and dragged it from the den, a fine little male fox, barely old enough to leave the den on its own, the eyes still bleary from the weeks spent in the dark. He tucked the fox into his coat pocket and buttoned the tab before reaching into the tunnel again and finding another cub, and another. One, two, three little foxes. Brim should have been there to practise her counting … as she ate them: one little fox cub, two little fox cubs …

Albert looked at the last cub and felt it tremble

as it tried to bury its face in his hand, searching for the security of its brother and sister's fur. Poor little thing, he thought, should bump it on the head really, a fox, a chicken killer, goose egg thief, should kill it, but … I can't.

The pads of the little paws were pink and soft as a baby's toes. How could you raise your hand to kill it, even though you knew it would grow into a killer itself? He couldn't do it and that was that. Should never have reached into the hole, should have let them die of starvation, would never have known the little fellows, should never have looked into their eyes and through to their tiny tremulous hearts, and after his thumb sought out the minute pulse he couldn't have killed them for all the tea in China.

CHOUGHS

'China,' the girl wrote, 'is a big country with a lot of people and they grow tea ... and rice.'

She looked at what she had written, fiddled with the pen, rotating the plastic tube between her thumb and forefinger. 'China.' Her mother said she should keep up her schooling, even though she was sick. Too sick to be outside.

She looked out the window. Seven birds waddled into the yard with a gait that made their tails sweep and bob. They seemed to be talking to each other, like women down at the shops.

'Maria, have you finished your assignment yet?' Her mother said as she bustled into the room, always something bordering on accusation in her voice.

'Yes,' Maria replied, knowing this answer would not be sufficient.

'Is this it? Just this, "China is a big …"'

'I was going to write more.'

'You were looking out the window.'

'What are those birds?'

'What birds?'

'Those ones, out there, talking to each other.'

Mrs Coniliopoulos went to the window trying to think of reasons why sick girls shouldn't waste time looking at birds. When do I ever get time to look out windows?

'They … they're crows … scavengers, peck the eyes out of lambs.'

'But they've got white on them.'

'Well, they're still scavengers, waltzing about, think they own the place. Anyway it's about time you finished the China assignment so I can take it up to the school. I don't want you falling behind. When you get well and go back …'

Maria stopped listening and clicked the Google icon on her computer. Birds, she typed, of Australia. Crow. She looked at the picture of the very bad crow. *Her* birds were not crows. Not ravens, either, or currawongs, or friar birds, or … Choughs, that's what they were, choughs. How were you supposed to say that? She scrolled down. Happy family birds. *The chough is a sociable bird that lives in close family groups and all members help …*

'Maria, that's not China,' her mother accused, looking over her shoulder, 'that's those crows.'

'They're choughs,' Maria said.

'Oh, Maria, please concentrate, I'm not doing this to be mean, darling, you know I just want …'

Mrs Coniliopoulos began wringing her hands and Maria knew from experience that the wringing would squeeze tears from her mother's eyes.

Maria looked out the window. Happy family birds.

Mrs Coniliopoulos stared at the top of her

daughter's head where the hair was thin, sick looking, from the chemotherapy. What can I do, what can I do? The woman wailed within her own heart, I'm a single mother and my daughter is …

'Maria, please, I'm begging you to finish the assignment, please, because when you get …'

Maria turned and looked squarely at her mother's face. She knew her mother was trying to do the right thing, trying to be the kind of mother that solved things, but instinctively she knew that her mother had only the vaguest idea what to do in most circumstances and since the illness had arrived she could only think about getting Maria to work. That's all the woman had ever done, that was the only solution she could think of to any difficulty in life. Work.

»→ * ←«

When Albert got back to the hut Brim was looking up at him, the hair standing up on the back of her neck at the smell of fox.

'Now, now, Brim, don't look at me like that, old girl, these is little baby foxes, pads as pink as geraniums, just like your own little babies. How would you like it if I grabbed up your own little pups and killed them?'

He sat on the chair and appealed to Brim. 'I pulled them outta the hole and soon as I saw 'em, that was it, couldn't raise a hand against them, their little hearts goin' pumpity pump, drumpity drump, bursting with the will to live … like all of us.'

He reached into his pocket and held the cubs in his own huge paw and they went as still as … well, as still as fox cubs terrified by the smell of man *and* dog and the dark ticking of a thing they'd never heard before. Albert's clock. Well, Albert's grandmother's clock really.

Brim looked up at Albert and sniffed the awful scent of fox and ducked her head down to nuzzle her pups to check that they had not been harmed by the dreadful presence of foxes. How many foxes? Lotsa foxes. She was too annoyed to count them, there was lotsa foxes and she didn't care for them one bit.

'Now, now, Brim, don't be like that, I've made a blue and now you've gotta help me. You're me dog and you've gotta help me, that's what mates do.'

He went down on his knee before his little ginger mate and held the cubs out to her. Her lip curled involuntarily but Albert beseeched her and she tried, she really did, she stretched forward to sniff the cubs but recoiled with her nostrils quivering, such an ugly, wild, unholy smell.

Unholy! What's unholy? Some living thing that is strange to you?

'Come on, Brim, you can see how little they are, you can see they're not weaned, they're starvin', poor little devils.'

Albert held a cub toward one of Brim's spare teats, while Brim's own pups were tumbled in dog sleep, all pink tummy and silken ear, all milky breath and mother warm.

The cub's nostrils quivered suddenly at the smell of milk. Wild milk, unholy milk, *dog* milk, but milk for all that and she hadn't been fed for four days, and her mother gone and her brother gone and now this big creature burying her in his pocket and this *dog* glaring at her ... but the milk, the *milk*, the lovely warm slippery milk. Her tongue made little darts from her lips, hungry for dog milk despite herself.

Albert lowered the little creature to the teat and Brim flinched as it took hold, her eyes widening with panic, fearful of the little foreigner, hating its ugly, narrow little head, not at all like her own babies with their blunt loveable faces, the most beautiful creatures to ever live.

What are you doing to me, Albert? Brim's eyes pleaded, because even though she could count she couldn't talk, it's a fox, Albert, a *fox*. One fox is one too many.

Albert watched the cub attach itself greedily, the pups too full of milk and sleep to notice, their fat pink tummies fit to burst. Albert brought out another cub and placed it beside its sister.

That's two foxes, Albert, *two*, Brim appealed, but Albert took no notice, bringing the last cub from his capacious pocket.

That's another one, Brim's eyes signalled alarm, that's … that's lotsa foxes.

But the foxes just suckled ferociously while Albert squatted down beside Brim and reassured her with a calming hand repeatedly following the curve of her brow to the base of her neck, strong, sure strokes pressing calm and acceptance into her heart. If Albert thought it was all right for a bitch to suckle a fox, lotsa foxes, then it must be all right. Why, even Rome was built by human babies suckled by a wolf. Dogs didn't learn much history but paid particular attention to the bits where dogs and wolves were involved.

DOGS AND DOXES

I'm forty-one years old, Vera Coniliopoulos thought as she watched the tortured breath of her daughter, groping through the suffocation of the hard chemicals sent to kill her cells, the good and the bad. Forty-one and my daughter is dying and no-one loves me.

It's not hard to be maudlin in the stifled light of a sick person's room, but in her heart Vera knew it was close enough to the truth to crush her spirit.

Vera was almost right but not quite because

Maria loved her mother. She admired her selflessness, a mother's great gift for uncompromised love. Even when it was needy love. She could admire that love, respect it, even if it smothered her like wads of cotton wool. The way they pack dolls in a toy shop. All satin and padding, like a coffin.

Vera struggled with her gloom. She knew she could slip in to it like a hand in a warm glove. She was aware of it, even allowed the word for it, self-pity, to rise in her mind like a bubble of gas in a swamp. But she is my life. And she knew that was wrong too. You can't bind your children to you so they *have* to love you, but the two can get confused. It can't be wrong to love your daughter so entirely and it can't be very wrong to want some in return.

What can I do? the woman asked herself. Nothing more than you can, God replied. Or Vera thought he did anyway. And it was some comfort. A little, because even inside the religion she'd known all her life Mrs Coniliopoulos had doubts. Grave doubts.

»→ * ←«

Soon the pups and cubs were old enough to stay in the hut while Brim resumed her supervision of Albert's work in the bush.

Each night when they returned from the ridge the pups would yip and squeal until Brim slumped onto the bag and they jostled each other to reach a teat, the three fox cubs slinking in behind them, already sensitive to their rank in the litter.

Brim was a good, healthy mother and all the pups and cubs flourished and became so boisterous in their tumbling fights that the more lightly built foxes had to be alert and nimble to avoid being squashed.

It was a strange sight to see them all snuggle into Brim at night, the four blunt-faced pups and the three arrow-headed cubs, each of them being given a good cleaning: ears, nose, eyes, bottoms, feet and last of all tummies, just for fun.

When they had grown strong and agile enough to get bored, Albert allowed them to follow their mother up the hill, lest he return one night to find the bedding all torn to bits and the kitchen pots upset.

They need not worry about the yellow-eyed goshawk because Brim prowled about the splitting camp, shadowing the pups and cubs, bristling if even a currawong got too close.

Albert chuckled to himself about the strangeness of it, seeing the little foxes who thought they were dogs tumbling about the clearing, sometimes spilling into the ashes at the edge of the fire and having their whiskers and ears dusted ash grey, as comical as anything he'd ever seen.

They were good hunters too. While the pups couldn't contain their enthusiasm, dashing after crickets and butterflies, making crazy leaping bounds at the taunting swallows, the fox cubs were sly little creepers and hiders, using the bracken and grasses to camouflage their outlines, only leaping out when they felt sure they could catch their prey.

But really, what could you do with a butterfly whose lightness and bouncing flight made it seem like hunting air? And the crickets who were easily caught but could make you leap a metre in the air with their sudden and frightening crick-it, crick-it? Or even worse the bug-eyed cicadas whose glistening, transparent wings tasted like cellophane and were most terrifying when they crook crook cricked into voice and soon set up such a drumming and insistent alarm that a fox's eyes might pop right out of its head?

Albert found himself laughing under his breath and Brim would glance up at him with mild reproof, burdened with her relentless vigil of looking after one, two … ah … and another one, two pups and one, two … ah … well, who cares, lotsa foxes. Do you know what it's like, Albert, she seemed to say, having eyes in the back of your head? Watching this one tumbling around the fire and upsetting the billy? This one chasing butterflies and falling off a log? That one with its head stuck in a jam tin? That one, no two, trying to gang up on the choughs? It's exhausting, that's what, so you look after them if you think it's that funny.

But Albert had his own work to do, and plenty of it. Hard yakka. Splitting out the green posts, heavy and slippery with sap. But he had to admit the frivolous antics of the pups and cubs made the day go quickly.

He was aware that other people might think him strange, being so fond of his animals and the bush creatures. All very well to go all dreamy and sooky watching the cubs being cleaned before bed, but what would other bushmen think? Foxes? The enemy. Some of them didn't look at Brim very kindly, either, despite the fact she was the best dog from Combienbar to Wangarabell. No, what some of them saw was the dingo in her, the enemy. Some people could find enemies everywhere. All Albert saw were living creatures, little animals of innocence.

He'd have to be careful when they got older and bolder, have to make sure they kept away from the other bushmen's camps. The pups would be all right because there were plenty who knew Brim's worth and any pup from her was sure to be sought after.

Her first litter had hardly been weaned before rough-bearded bushmen and practical country women came to stand about Albert's campfire to watch the pups, making their claim for one or the other depending on which they perceived would best meet their needs.

Some wanted a good watchdog and so they looked for a bright eye and a keen bark; some wanted a bold dog who would be good around sheep and cows; the women often wanted a trainable dog, a pup that you could teach to leave the chooks alone and to let babies pull their ears and inspect their teeth.

Mrs Carbone had a baby boy who, thinking the goat was his brother, wanted to see why he was wearing a ridiculous false beard, and, of course, ended up being butted head over heels into the chicken poo. Mrs Carbone knew any dog she brought home would have to tolerate close inspection with gentle patience.

One of the bushmen kept his requirements to himself but chose the fattest and laziest pup out of Brim's first litter. Cranky Dave kept himself to himself and his opinions were his own. People thought he was a grumpy old coot but in truth he was a shy man, and if he grunted at you when you said good morning it was because he flushed so red with embarrassment his lips were as useful for speech as an earthworm for a tent peg.

'That one,' he told Albert at last.

'That one?' Albert said, 'well, that's lucky isn't it, Dave?' Albert never used his nickname out of politeness and, to be honest, decency, because Dave wasn't a bad bloke, just a bit quiet and serious. 'That's lucky indeed, old mate, because that's the only one left.'

'I knew that,' Dave grumbled, 'but it's the one I want.' So he went off a happy man because he'd chosen a fat and happy pup. He figured that a fat pup would be the warmest and warmest was what he wanted. He secretly christened her Queenie, well Queenie Bush Bess Lovelock to be exact. He'd have to keep the full name a secret because Lovelock was Dave's surname, and you'd have to keep *that* secret wouldn't you? No-one knew about Lovelock, not even Albert who Dave considered a friend.

You didn't get far in the bush world of cattlemen and splitters with a name like Lovelock. Especially if you weren't a slap-on-the-back sort of mate, a few-quick-beers-before-the-missus-finds-out sort of fellow. No, that sort of bloke would laugh in the face of a man called Lovelock.

Better to be called Carbone or Mirrabella. Even the Ah Mats got away with their foreign-sounding name most of the time. No-one bothered the publican, Plowman; the postman, Goodchild, survived all right; and even Mrs Cartright-Sellers escaped much ribbing, but that was because she had a black cat and rumour had it that she was a witch, a rumour much assisted by the prominent mole on her nose and her habit of sweeping the veranda with a broom made of willow wands.

Little Gordon Baldock received his most attentive audience ever when he told people he'd seen her flying across the sky in front of the moon. But Gordon was the sort of kid who just liked to see other people in trouble. A shame about that but there you are.

Yes, people left Mrs Cartright-Sellers to herself but Dave wasn't going to risk people finding out about the Lovelock bit. He got his mail delivered to Dave, Boulder Creek Camp, near Narkoonjee.

Dave wanted a fat, warm pup because he was a soft sort of man, which no-one knew, and a lonely man, about which no-one cared, or so it seemed to Dave. He wanted a fat, warm pup to climb in under his old army blanket and settle itself behind the small of his back because his hut could be fearful cold in winter and his arthritis was beginning to give him gyp. He also wanted the company of a fellow living creature. Someone to talk to while he rubbed her little fat silken ears with his rough timber cutter's fingers.

Yes, Dave had the right dog. When he stroked the perfect dome of her little head he marvelled at the perfection of creation. He'd lift her baby-pink feet, smell the warm nuttiness of them and kiss her between the eyes when she went all dozy in front of the fire.

He found something strange in his chest one lunch time when she paddled up to him in her tumbly clumsy puppy way and crawled onto his lap. Very strange sort of feeling in his chest. He was chuckling. Laughing at the ridiculous little dog. What a strange sensation laughing is, especially if you haven't been able to do it for a while.

Oh, he loved that Queenie Bess and she loved

him. And kept him warm. And loved. And everyone needs that, someone to think they're really special.

Now the men and women of the forest gathered around Brim's second litter and the pups gradually left: one to mind sheep; another to look after little Gabby Arnold because he was stuck in a wheelchair, poor blighter; another to keep an old dog company; one just to be an ordinary sort of dog; and the last to get run over by a truck because no-one in the Howard house had time or love enough to stop it chasing cars.

And so there were only fox cubs left. One, two … er … oh, you know how many foxes were left, lotsa the silly little coots.

Like any mother, Brim was distraught when the pups were taken from her, but Albert was the boss in her world and she was reassured by his love. To say that she was a reluctant mother of the remaining fox cubs is not quite correct. The foxes loved her and believed she was their mother; they thought of themselves as dogs. And while Brim was conscientious, she seemed slightly alarmed by them, unnerved by their foxy behaviour.

The look of bewilderment never left her face. She would let them drink and dutifully clean their faces and fur with a thoroughness that was out of her control, but whenever they gave their strange little fox yips and whines the poor dingo flinched in alarm.

Nevertheless she grew them up and tried to teach them how to be good dogs. The foxes loved their mother and tried to be just like her, but they weren't.

Brim liked to give her territory a good sniff every morning and the foxes followed suit, but the urge to hunt anything that moved was irresistible. They ate grasshoppers and worms, quail chicks and lizards, anything they could sniff out with their sharp little noses. Brim looked on amazed and at times seemed a little repulsed.

All baby animals grow up and their most endearing traits — their clumsiness, their playfulness and their ability to fall asleep in the most unlikely places — were replaced by stealth and wariness, latent aggression and an altogether more serious outlook on life.

Gradually the foxes extended their range and the time they spent away from Brim and each other. The two females in particular seemed to be itching to explore as far as they could, sometimes not returning to the hut until dusk was well advanced. Soon they'd be hunting in the dark. As foxes do.

But not Fog. The boy had all the slinky stealth and hunting lust of his sisters but he was always the first to seek out Brim and rest in the shade with her or find Albert's coat and try to get back in the pocket to sleep, even though he was now far too big.

The smell of the coat was important to Fog, almost as if he remembered being bundled in there by the old man's hands all those months ago. Whenever Albert wore the coat Fog would try to climb onto his lap. If he took the coat off Fog would sleep on it. Brim was never far from the coat either. She knew her job was to guard Albert first and his things second. If Albert didn't want her under his feet while he split timber Brim would always go back to sit beside his coat or the lunch things. The vixens would get bored almost immediately and slope off into the forest, but when Albert looked around from his work Brim was always watching him as she lay with jaw resting on paws … And more often than not Fog was asleep on his coat.

One warm evening when the moon was three-quarters full and rose just after sunset the vixens didn't come home.

Albert looked for them the next day although he wasn't really expecting their return, but he wanted to reassure himself that they hadn't fallen victim to wild dogs or eagles.

No, they'd just gone off. Off to be wild, Albert thought with approval, not without a pang of loss, because they were charming animals, a delight to have around with their bright-eyed intelligence and outright beauty.

They'd gone because they were fully weaned and independent. Why Fog remained was a mystery. Were the males slower to develop and leave home or was there something else?

Brim took to sleeping on Albert's bed, as much to ease her arthritis as anything, but perhaps also to declare her rights above those of Fog, a mere fox.

A fox or a dox? Albert wondered, looking at the animal lying in front of the wood stove. Even though the evenings were warm Fog liked to be near the stove or more particularly the coat, which Albert hung on the back of his fireside chair whenever he came inside.

It was a peculiar family. Albert found there were plenty of people who disapproved, most of whom had never even seen Fog, but this didn't stop them from accusing the dox of having stolen their chickens and ducklings.

Unlike his two wild sisters Fog hardly went anywhere on his own. He learnt to be content with whatever food Albert provided, and he was happiest when Albert wore his coat. Fog was a homely dox.

But people can't abide anything different and many can't relax until the difference is destroyed. Fog would have got blamed if the cat had kittens.

As far as Albert was concerned Fog had decided he was a dox and that was good enough for Albert. Albert's heart was a very decent piece of machinery.

I know this is a story and the hero of a story usually has to be good, kind, brave and good-looking, but the truth of the matter is that while Albert was demonstrably good and kind, in his mind they were just habits he couldn't break. And as for courage, how do you know if you've got it until you need it?

But Albert certainly was not handsome, teetering on the edge of ugliness — if it weren't for his smile. He definitely was not young, and to be a respectable hero you have to be young. But the truth is that Albert isn't the hero. He's just a kind man and I don't know about you, but I reckon that's a good-enough reason to include anyone in a story — even an old man whose blunt features could be described as plain if not a bit coarse.

But if you'd met Albert, as I have done, you might see Albert's face as interesting. Because if a person can't have a beautiful face they can make their face interesting by gazing out of it with intelligence and kindness. When I first saw Albert's face that's what I saw, not the crooked nose, craggy jaw and dodgy teeth, but how he quizzed me with those kindly dark eyes, looked into my soul, looking for *my* goodness.

I'm sticking up for Albert because he suffered other people's unkindness with never a mean remark in return, never a bad deed done to make his detractors fall on their face. Once those fox cubs had licked his fingers, mewled in his ear and nuzzled his neck, he could no more ignore their plight than hurt any human.

Sometimes, after Albert had cleaned up the evening dishes and poured himself a big mug of tea, he'd stare into the firebox of his stove and more often than not catch the earnest gaze of Fog, searching his face with the devotion of a dog and the acute enquiry of a fox.

'So, Fog, my dox, what do you think about the world and its people?'

Fog studied Albert's face and considered the question but said nothing.

'You see, my young dox-cub-pup, there are people who will hate you simply because someone else said you were to be hated. Never seen you before, never sat by the fire and had a chat with you, just determined to be afraid of you and hate you because you're different.'

Albert drained his tea. Fog thought Albert made a little more noise sipping his tea than was entirely necessary and felt sure there was no need for him to dunk his nose in it while he was at it. It was a fairly big nose, Albert's, and as we've just discussed his face, you get the picture. But have you ever seen a fox with dirty whiskers? Fog's point entirely.

Fog wasn't judging Albert, but foxes are so neat in their habits that the gorging and slobbering that some dogs and humans went in for remained an unpleasant surprise. Brim was neat and finicky for a dog but still managed to get more of her dinner on her whiskers and chops than Fog thought becoming. Still, he tolerated that — she was his mother.

Brim's summer habit of sleeping on Albert's bed became a very determined winter habit. She wasn't a young dog, the years were taking their toll, and on some particularly frosty mornings she feigned profound sleep and forgetfulness so that it was just Fog who escorted Albert into the forest to watch over the lunchbox and his coat.

Brim would be waiting in front of the hut when they returned with an air of sham irritation that they hadn't waited that extra one or two or … lotsa minutes for her to get ready so that she could have left with them in the morning.

She wagged her tail and inspected Fog, sniffed the axes, the lunchbox and Albert's trousers to make sure nothing had gone awry in her absence, but ah, the luxury of dozing away by the fire with only the baleful stare of the owl to reprimand her. And it was nearly tea time already! Life was good.

BIRTHDAYS

One Sunday morning Fog and Brim lay in the sun beside Albert's outside chair where he liked to drink his third cuppa. Suddenly the dog and dox pricked their ears and looked toward the forest path with tension and expectation. Brim began a couple of uncertain wags of her tail before remembering that she was a fierce guard dog and bristling the hair about her neck in a show of threat. But soon she could not restrain her tail because she felt sure she knew who was coming.

Cranky Dave stepped into the clearing with his perennial grumpy self-effacement, Queenie Bess heeling beside him. Brim dashed forward and gave the nervous young dog such a sniffing exploration that anyone would have been a bit intimidated.

'She's four,' Cranky Dave announced, as if everyone should know exactly what he meant. 'Queenie Bess, she's four today. She wanted to come for her birthday.'

Blimey, Albert thought, he's got worse.

'Ah, now that's good, Dave, glad to hear it. Almost slipped me mind when the pups were born.'

Dave was staring at Fog who was sitting up like a good dox, all attention and good manners. But it didn't matter which way you looked at it, he was still a fox.

'That fox there looks pretty tame, Albert.'

Albert passed Dave a good strong cup of tea, marvelling at the extent of Dave's new found sociability. 'Yes, very quiet, doesn't worry the birds and animals, comes to work every day, never misses a beat.'

'So, what are you going to do with him?'

'Nothing, he's a mate. Just like your Queenie.'

'Oh,' said Dave thinking about it for a moment and deciding that if Albert thought there was no harm in it then there probably wasn't. 'Well, that's good then, to have a mate.'

The two men sat surrounded by the two dogs and the fox and drank their tea in companionable silence. Dave seemed to relax and expand. It's true that his burst of conversation had dried up but he was like a man practising having a friend. He sat forward in his chair cradling the cup in his big hands and settling his feet in a more relaxed position.

'It's good to catch up, Dave,' Albert said at last, 'have a cuppa and a chat.'

Dave made a bit of a noise in his nose that sounded like agreement and shuffled his feet.

'Here,' Dave said after a long silence, 'I brought you this. For your fox.' He handed Albert a small parcel.

Albert peeled the coloured paper off carefully. He didn't get many wrapped parcels so he wasn't going to rush this one. He wanted to show his friend he appreciated it. Whatever it was.

Inside he found a collar made from thongs of kangaroo hide, and in a neat capsule of leather Dave had secured a red stone the size of a two dollar coin.

'It's not a real ruby,' Dave rushed and fumbled his explanation, 'garnet, it's garnet. I found a big one in the creek and kind of cut it on me wheel. Bit rough but it shines all right.'

Albert turned the collar in his hands and saw that Dave, Crazy Dave, had cut holes in either side of the pocket that clasped the gemstone so that light could shine through. It was a work of art, of friendship, of love.

'Me an' Queenie thought ya fox might like it.'

'He's called Fog. I reckon he's a dox.'

'Dox?' Dave let it tumble through his mind, 'like a sorta cross between a dog and a fox?'

'Yes, a dox. He's a good dox, don't ya reckon?'

'Yeah, yeah, I do. Like my Queenie here, real good. I come ta thank ya for the pup, Albert. I got no money so me an' Queenie thought a collar for the … dox would kinda say … you know, thanks.'

'Well, thank you, Dave, I'm just glad ya like the dog. Glad to see Brim's pup well cared for and healthy.'

'She's a mate, see, goes everywhere with me. Keeps me company at work, someone to talk to — ' His jaw clamped shut and his eyes sparkled with panic. He hadn't meant to say that he talked to the dog like a person, like *someone*. That was the problem with conversations. You sometimes said things that got you into trouble. After all the years of being the butt of smarter men's jokes he'd developed the habit of saying almost nothing in company.

Albert saw the panic in Dave's eyes and realised he hadn't meant to expose his dreadful secret of talking to an animal.

'Oh, they like a bit of a yarn, don't they?' Albert said. 'Even the dox here likes to hear a story or two, and the maggies and pigeons, they stick their head on the side an' listen as long as I've got stories to tell.'

Dave stared at Albert and relaxed in his chair

but said very little else. He accepted another cup of tea and a bit of companionable silence while he stroked Fog's head tentatively, thoughtfully.

Before long he stood, thanked Albert for the tea, accepted his thanks for the collar with a grunt that would have sounded rude if you didn't know him, and then stalked into the forest like a shambling scarecrow on the loose. He would have looked alarming if there hadn't been a completely normal dog trotting faithfully by his side.

»⟩ * ⟨«

Maria lay on her side, her damp hair sticking to her face like spider webs. She was too weak to lift a hand to tuck it behind her ear. She was watching Discovery Channel again. Otters. Beautiful slinky, swimmy mammals. Their undulating movement was like unrestrained joy. The joy of being alive. And that made Maria's heart sink.

Her mother did everything the nurse asked, believed everything she said. Too cold to risk going outside in the sun. Even if it was almost summer. There's a breeze the nurse proclaimed and that was that. Discovery Channel. Maria had pleaded with them both.

'Maybe tomorrow,' Mrs Coniliopoulos cajoled, 'maybe the chemo will have worn off enough. Just one more day.'

'Promise.'

'If the nurse …'

Maria tried to turn away but couldn't. Her eyes strayed back to giraffes nibbling the foliage off African thorn bushes, like construction cranes having afternoon tea. Delicate.

'Please, Maria, just one more day, and we'll ask …'

Nurse, nurse, curse the nurse, Maria thought. No-one who prefers being inside can ever understand how suffocating it is for people who like being *out*side.

One more day, just one more day, she thought and wondered with brooding gloom if giraffes ever got a thorn up their nose. One more day.

SPINEBILLS

Just because Brim missed going to work some frosty mornings doesn't mean her diligence had evaporated. Most mornings she watched for the signs of Albert's departure and was by his side when he stepped into the forest.

But there were some mornings when she just didn't feel like it. Occasionally her hips would play up or she would sigh once too often, glance about the comforts of the hut and decide it would be too hot, too cold or too far for an ageing lady to be gallivanting about on the mountain. And Fog was there to make sure Albert was looked after. Just as well … there had to be some use for a dox.

Albert wondered if there would come a time when he too couldn't drag himself from the hut to go to work. Not *if,* he supposed, but *when.*

Still, he was fit and it was an absolute pleasure to be out in the bush. The work was hard but he was used to it and it was satisfying to see the sweet slippery posts leap out of the log after he'd split them out with the wedges. He usually had two mates, Fog and Brim, but not this morning. It was one of Brim's rostered days off. He was thinking this over as he drank his tea at smoko and entertained the devilish thought of having another one.

The tree he was splitting had a dense twisty grain. Most of what he cut was stringy bark but this tree was a kind of hybrid. He came across them from time to time and they usually made splitting difficult. They had a tight strong grain with a bit of a wave in it that prevented the log from splitting freely.

So, another cup of tea before he set about the task with his wedges and mallet.

He allowed his eye to roam about the clearing. There was usually something to catch his interest. When he arrived this morning he'd watched an echidna breaking open an ants' nest, peering around comically from time to time in its nearsightedness. Albert supposed we'd all be near-sighted if we spent our life with our snouts in a hole looking for ants.

And look at that, one of his favourite birds, the eastern spinebill, was good enough to keep him company right on smoko. He'd *have* to have that second cuppa now.

They were a beautiful bird, fine curved beak like an ebony darning needle and the most elegant costume. The eyes were deep chestnut and the black cap on the head continued as two narrow ribbons on either side of its chest. Above the ribbons it had a snowy white vest and below the beak a bib of cinnamon. The nape and belly were the same colour. Some people preferred the showy crimson rosella or the bold and vain golden whistler; others raved about the prima donna lyrebird or the theatrical bowerbird. Albert loved them all but the spinebill was so neat and its voice so clear and spirited it always cheered him to hear it.

One of the most charming things about the bird was the way it could hover in front of a flower to extract nectar with its fine curved bill, just like a humming bird. He never got sick of watching it and this morning it put on a great display, hovering from flower to flower of a mountain grevillea.

At last Albert turned his eye reluctantly to the log waiting for him. Fog followed his gaze and dropped down onto the old man's coat, reading the signs that the splitting was about to begin and his job was to guard the lunch box.

Albert slapped his hands on his knees, pushed himself up from the stump and approached the log with resolute determination.

He tapped the first wedge in and sap oozed from around the opening it made. Mmm, he thought, sappy little critter, must be all that rain we've had over winter, got a real good sap flow going.

He tapped in a second wedge and gradually opened a crack through the middle of the log and stood back to examine it.

'Bit slippery this one, Fog. They're a bit like that after rain. Don't like the way the wedges keep slipping. I'll put a couple of extra ones in the side to keep it open, what do you reckon?'

Fog was used to being consulted about Albert's progress. He cocked his head on one side, yes, probably a good idea, he thought, not knowing a hell of a lot about fenceposts and timber.

Albert worked away carefully, gradually opening a yawning gap at the end of the log. The wedges kept slipping in the sluice of sap, one even popped straight out and flew ten metres before it crashed into a currant bush. Albert always made sure his campfire and lunch box were off to one side so that an event like that didn't hurt Brim or Fog.

At last he had the log to the point where he'd be able to drive in his largest wedge and split the entire log in half. But just as he tapped it in one of the side wedges loosened and slipped into the jaws of the log.

He stood back and looked at it. He'd have to get it out. Couldn't risk it being fired out like a missile if the log snapped back into place.

He knelt beside the log and reached between the gaping jaws but couldn't quite reach the wedge. So he got down on both knees and reached in a little further. But as he did so the hammer he was carrying in his other hand bumped the main wedge, which spat from the log like a vicious little assassin, and the log slammed shut on Albert's arm.

His reflex was to wrench his arm free but he was too late and instead was flung down beside the log, the hammer spinning from the grasp of his free hand.

He'd heard of this happening. It wasn't good. He'd worked hard to avoid it ever happening, but it had and now he was trapped. Think clearly now, Albert. Which wasn't as easy as it sounded because the pain in his arm was as if a blowtorch was strafing it with a naked flame.

Fog leapt to his feet in alarm. He didn't like those logs one bit. He was a smart dox but had never worked out why Albert bothered with them at all.

Albert twisted himself about so that he was kneeling beside the log. He tugged at his arm but knew exactly what the result would be. Useless. He'd have to try and drive a wedge in beside his arm to open the jaws of the log again. He could see that the hammer was out of reach but there was one wedge not too far away, and, of course, the one he still grasped in his trapped hand.

He turned to look at Fog. The dox was staring at him, waiting to see what Albert would do. Or say.

'What are ya like at playing fetch, eh?'

Fog tipped his head to one side trying to figure out what Albert was talking about.

'Get the hammer, Fog. Can ya, mate? Can ya get the hammer for me?'

The dox just stared in an anguish of incomprehension. He knew Albert was in trouble and needed him to do something, but what?

Albert tried to encourage Fog by throwing sticks but he just looked at the stick in disbelief. He was a dox, he didn't chase sticks. What's the point, he thought, I'll get the stick and you'll just throw it away again.

The pain was killing Albert and the day was getting hotter. He slumped forward onto the log to rest and think. Think. Think. What to do.

>>*«

He drifted in and out of consciousness as the heat of the afternoon gave way to evening. Fog sat by him while he slept but when Albert woke and repeated his calls of 'Get the hammer, Fog. Fetch the hammer, Fog', it had frustrated the dox to such an extent that he retreated to the coat to think. When he thought he'd worked it out Fog dragged the lunch box over to Albert. And when that didn't fix things, the coat. If he puts the coat on he'll get his arm back!

'Ah, yer a good dox, Fog, yer a very good dox, but ya not too good at English are ya?' Albert rubbed the dox between his pointy red ears and Fog was greatly pleased, thinking he'd guessed what Albert needed him to do.

Albert ate a tiny square of boiled fruitcake and

had a sip of milk from the small jar. He looked across to the campfire but knew the billy was empty because he'd had that second cup of tea. He'd have to be careful with the jar of milk, it was all he had.

He was in a jam. Literally. No-one would think to search for him. Brim would come looking for him eventually but her grasp of language was not much better than Fog's. Oh, she could count a bit but that didn't mean she'd understand about getting the hammer.

The thought that he might die beside the log loomed like a dark shroud. Bloomin' log. Should have left it to season a bit, dry out before he split it up. Never mind, it's done now, nothing for it but to try and think.

He didn't like the way his whole arm had gone numb and it alarmed him that he kept blacking out. He was thirsty, that was the problem. He'd lain there in the sun all day with just a small jar of milk to drink … and it was all but curdled. He was in trouble.

Fog paced about him trying to work out why he

didn't get up and go home. It was *tea* time! You're
hungry, I'm hungry, let's go and get some *tea*!
The dox scratched at the ground beside Albert as
darkness crept between the trees. Come on Albert,
come on, let's go home.

But now Albert spent more time unconscious
than awake and Fog looked at him anxiously.
Animals, particularly dogs, but also doxes, sense
when another animal is failing. They actually
hear the rhythm of the heart, smell the stress of
the body struggling to keep itself alive. Fog knew
Albert was in real trouble.

All at once the dox set its ears toward his owner
in a moment of inspiration and startling clarity,
spun on his little foxy paws and left the clearing in
a mad leaping dash like a piece of ribbon dancing
through the bush. They're noiseless, foxes, they
run with an undulating fluidity. Doxes are the
same. Fog was gone in a flash of white tail tip,
disappearing like the mist of his name.

Crazy Dave heard the scraping at the door and
expected to see Dug, the wombat he'd reared as
an orphan. Dug turned up occasionally wanting a

scratch and a piece of apple, and Dave opened the door ready to berate him for ripping his door to bits. He recoiled in shock on seeing a fox looking up at him. Automatically he reached for the gun behind the door but then the light from the kerosene lamp shone richly on the garnet in the fox's collar. It wasn't a fox at all, it was a dox.

'Fog ol' fella, what's up?' Dave spoke kindly to the dox, being much better at conversation with animals than people. The young dox looked at him keenly then looked back towards the forest track.

'Albert is it? Crook?' Dave grabbed his coat and called Queenie to the door. Fog gave his step-sister a perfunctory greeting and stepped toward the track.

Illness or accident were the things all the old bushmen feared: any incapacitation, broken leg, or any sickness that prevented you from moving. You were vulnerable in the bush. Sometimes even your best mate, your dog, couldn't help. But perhaps a dox might.

Dave brought his lamp and followed Fog and Queenie as they trotted ahead. It was pitch dark in the forest and Fog was setting such a brisk pace that Dave almost missed the turnoff. He'd been expecting to follow the track all the way to Albert's hut but Fog turned off and waited until he was sure Dave was following.

In silence, but for the crunch of Dave's boots on forest litter, they climbed the hillside and as Dave understood the direction they were taking he felt an awful dread. A forest accident was the worst of all bushmen's fears. Falling trees caused horrible injuries and Dave wasn't looking forward to finding his friend beneath one. Yes, he'd unconsciously used the word friend. Albert was his friend, in an exclusive club of one.

When they entered the clearing Dave looked about for the widow-maker, the maverick tree that had trapped or killed his mate and, at first, looked past the log in the centre of the clearing.

But Fog ran straight to it and began tugging at something and Dave saw the man slumped across the log. As he moved closer he saw how Albert's arm was trapped.

'Jesus,' he breathed. He wasn't a religious

man, Dave, but the utterance of that name came naturally in the circumstances. He wasn't the first man to look for divine help when facing a crisis beyond his own powers.

Albert was unconscious but not dead. Yet. Dave could see the merest movement of the shoulders as his old mate's lungs pushed him ever so slightly away from the log. But the breaths were slow and shallow.

A nightjar called, its weird whooping chuckle rippling and looping through the starlit clearing. Enough to wake the ... Dave felt Albert's pulse and the old man murmured.

Peering about Dave was able to find the wedges and the hammer. He tapped in a wedge with cautious blows and Albert moaned and protested in delirium.

Dave went to the end of the log and tapped in two more wedges and gradually opened the split log. Another wedge on the opposite side, a tap or two of the wedge near Albert's elbow, and finally the log was opened sufficiently for him to draw his friend's arm from the maw of gaping wood.

Dave inspected Albert's arm more closely. He could see the horrible swelling and bruising.

Suddenly Albert tugged his arm away.

'Look out, look out,' Albert cried so loudly that the nightjar was silenced as if a knife had cut his throat.

Albert's eyes opened and he stared uncomprehendingly at Dave.

'Get the hammer,' he growled urgently but then relaxed as he focused on his arm. Free of the log. He collapsed back into unconsciousness.

Freed from its compression, Albert's arm continued swelling alarmingly. Dave's head flipped through the various elements of the predicament and, after examining all the problems and the few things he possessed to solve them, his mind cleared as crisp as moonlight.

They had no vehicle, no track on which one could travel anyway, no horse, no phone, and no hope of any help arriving. Albert was suffering from shock and exposure and probably fractures and bleeding within his arm, and may not survive until dawn.

They were miles from the only doctor and there was only one way Albert was going to get there: Dave was going to have to carry him.

He hauled his friend onto his back and set off on the track that would take them to the log crossing at the river. Fog and Queenie trotted along with Dave, one in front and one behind, as if they'd already worked out their positions.

Dave was strong but Albert was a big, heavy man and in his semi-consciousness was difficult to carry. He lolled like a dead sheep. Dave had to grab the shirt above Albert's good shoulder with one hand and crook an arm below his mate's right leg and they managed that way but it was a terribly unbalanced load. Dave's muscles burned with fire and Albert's breath came in coarse, pained rasps.

Still, Dave plugged on. His arms screamed for relief but Dave refused their plea. He had only one human friend and that man was dying. Dave would never forgive himself if his mate died while he was resting in his arms. By the time he got to the river he was done in.

Tiger Carter had a house on the bank of the

river. Maybe he would help. Albert was Tiger's cousin but Tiger's kids were some of the bunch that jeered at Dave.

He bent to lift Albert again but he could hardly budge the unconscious man, his arms had seized up with the effort. He'd *have* to go to Carter's. They still had to get over the range and there was no way Dave could do it without help.

Carter had horses. Dave swallowed his shyness, lugged Albert onto his back again and started down the lane leading to Tiger Carter's house.

Tiger was one of those blokes who could do anything. Like Dave, he'd hardly set foot inside a school but he managed to support his family with hard work and inventiveness. He fished the river for yabbies and perch, kept bees and tended a massive orchard and vegetable garden. Tiger cut his own hay for the horses and all the kids chipped in to help sell the produce. The family ate well but had to scratch together an income from what they could sell to the neighbouring farms. The kids were kind of wild and Dave was terrified of them, but hopefully they'd be asleep.

He knocked on the door and thirty dogs set up a hullabaloo like you'd hear in the halls of hell. Dave heard shouts and footsteps and then the door scraped open and Tiger's shotgun levelled itself at Dave's chest.

'What's all the racket out here?' Tiger demanded, despite the fact that all the noise was inside the house.

'That's me cousin,' he blurted as the hall light fell on Albert's face slumped over Dave's shoulder. 'What's up? What's happened to him?' Finally Tiger recognised Dave. 'Oh, it's you Cra– ... Dave, didn't recognise you in the dark, mate. Quick, come in. What's up with Albert?'

'He got his arm caught in a log. He's gone an' blacked out. I've gotta get him to the hospital.'

'Hospital?'

'He's real crook. His pulse has got real faint, you'll have to help me. We've gotta get over the range.'

Yes, Tiger thought, the only way to get to the bush nurse quickly was to go over the top of Blast Pass. They'd need the horses.

'Hang on, Dave, I'll get young Col to saddle up some horses. Here, put this coat on me cousin and meet me around at the stable.' He turned inside, yelling out for Colin, which set the dogs off again. It was bedlam.

By the time Dave got to the stables Colin had one horse already saddled. The boy eyed Dave warily, embarrassed in front of the man he and his mates taunted every time they saw him. Colin handled the horse tack like he'd done it a thousand times. Soon all three horses were ready.

'What happened to Uncle Albert?' Colin asked at last, acting as if he hardly knew Dave.

'Got his arm trapped.'

'Up on his timber block?'

'Yes.'

'And you carried him all the way?'

'Yes.'

Colin knew about hard work. He'd seen the enormous labours of his parents, he'd been hauling firewood and fishnets himself since he was six. He understood the superhuman effort of carrying a big man all that way through the bush.

'I'm comin' too,' said Tiger dragging on a coat and handing a drizabone to Dave. 'Better put this on, mate, it's gunna be wet as hell goin' over the ridge. Should try and get one on Albert too or he'll freeze.'

Tiger had six horses but only three of them were up to making the top of the range so he had to ride his stallion, the failed racehorse Fair Go who he'd saved from the knackery. Fair Go was a terrifically willing horse but had never got over the idea that every time someone mounted him it was race time. Tiger had his hands full keeping him in check.

They'd tried to tie Albert onto Boots's saddle but he kept slipping to one side. Dave had to bring the old mare Sparkle alongside so that he could clutch his mate's coat and hold him in position. It'd be better if the stallion could draw alongside too but Tiger couldn't trust Fair Go to tolerate being so close to Sparkle and Boots. The presence of two dogs, well, one dog and another thing Tiger could swear was a fox, was spooking Fair Go enough as it was.

'We're in for it, Dave. Have a look at the moon,

she's on her back and the wind is getting up. It'll be hell up on the ridge.'

Even though it was almost summer the temperature had plummeted in front of a cold change and up on the ridge the wind would rip the temperature down another ten degrees. The sky had gone a weird bottle-green colour noticeable even by moonlight.

'Gees, we're gunna cop it all right. How's Albert goin'? It's gunna be rough on him later.'

Dave didn't answer. It was all he could do to hold his mate in the saddle. His left arm was killing him.

Suddenly the wind changed its tone to a banshee wail that whined through the limbs of the mountain gums crouching on the pass. It whistled like a kadaitcha through the bridle rings, spooking the horses further on top of their misgivings at riding at night in such stormy weather.

As they neared the top of the mountain ridge the trees gave way to low blasted heath and the wind roared in their ears so that it was impossible to hear anything anyone said.

'We'll have to canter, we'll be frozen in our

blessed saddles otherwise. I'll have to bring Fair Go up beside you. You'll never hold onto Albert on your own.'

Dave heard none of this but he knew what they had to do. At the top of the ridge the wind shrieked at them, biting at their faces and hands, and dragging at the horses' lips so they appeared to be grimacing in pain. The sudden cold was unbelievable. It felt like their flesh was lashed by ice. A sudden flurry of sleet pelted them with sharp and venomous needles. Fog and Queenie trotted as close to the heels of the horses as they dared, gaining a little protection in the lee of the horses' bulk.

Then a strange thing happened. Despite the abysmal conditions, the close proximity of other horses, and a dog and fox on his heels, Fair Go ranged alongside Boots and fell into perfect stride with both Boots and Sparkle. He kept his flank pressed to Albert's leg and never moved a centimetre closer or further away.

In perfect synchrony in that frightful cacophony of wind and sleet, the three horses crested the ridge stride for stride and plunged across it and down the other side, their very breaths hhrrumphing and crumping in rhythm.

'By geez,' Tiger remarked to himself, 'this bloomin' old racehorse knows what's goin' on. He thinks he's an ambulance.'

The three horses descended the mountain path in tight formation, the dog and dox never veering in their path behind them. Even in the relative shelter of the blunt mountain gums, the tempest still wailed about them and speech was useless. Not that that ever stopped Tiger.

'Gorn yer a good horse, Fair Go. Tell yer what, mate, I'm real impressed. Next time I go to give you a serve for yer excitable manners, just you remind me of this night. The night ya saved me cousin.' Tiger glanced across at Albert's ashen face half smothered in the collar of the weatherproof coat. 'If he's saved.'

At last the hooves clattered on the harder roads leading into the town. Some of the townspeople, woken by the moaning wind, heard the percussion of perfectly synchronised horses hoofs riding through the storm. Lydia Labertouche stared at her ceiling thinking, 'the ghostly horsemen came riding, riding, through wind and storm came riding', but even budding young poets can fall asleep in the middle of a poem — and she did.

The horses wheeled into the Bush Nursing Centre carpark and without a word two of the riders dismounted and hauled the third from his horse.

'Dave, I'll find a paddock for Sparkle and leave her there. Bring her back when you can. I've gotta get back to do the milking. Look after me cousin, won't ya.' Tiger looked at Albert with concern but he knew he couldn't stay and wait for the nurse. His cows would already be dawdling in to the dairy. He had to get back.

Dave just nodded and dragged Albert to the front door.

The Bush Nursing Centre was an old building no larger than a biggish house. It was four in the morning, a time when the only nurse on duty had her quiet time, her version of afternoon tea. She wasn't happy to hear banging at the door.

Dave could hear her grumbling even above his own laboured breaths and Albert's painful gasps.

'I'm coming … Middle of the night … Who would be making so much … ? What is it?' she demanded as she flung open the door.

Her eyes roamed over the scraggy old beast with an even scraggier old beast in his arms. Drunks, wouldn't you know it. Of all the … She looked closer and realised that they were just ordinary old bushmen, but that knowledge didn't do much to improve her humour. She'd been a bush nurse for twenty years and seen enough smelly old wrecks crawling out of the bush on their last legs.

'Don't bring your drunken mates in here and …' she began, about to give them a dressing down in her best matronly voice, when her eyes fell on Fog.

BUSH NURSE

'Ahhhhhhh!' she screamed, 'A wolf, a wolf, a ... a ... *fox*!'

Dave was beyond fright. He had to rest his arms.

'Shush, don't be stupid,' he said steadily, 'it's a dox, as anyone can see. Look, out of the way, I've got a sick man here.' Involuntarily Nurse Foran stepped aside, surprised at having been told to shush for the first time in her adult life. She quickly regained her poise and squared her shoulders ready to put this old weasel in his place, but he staggered past her and stumped along the corridor peering into the rooms to his left and right and, before she could stop him, he'd lowered Albert onto a freshly made bed.

'You can't … ' Nurse Foran began but the filthy bushman turned on her with mad glittering eyes.

'Shush,' he said, 'this man is nearly dead.' The nurse wasn't going to put up with this insolence and was about to deliver Hygiene Lesson Two when she realised that not only did she have two derelict bushmen in her hospital but the fox was in there too, and preparing to bite the patient's hand.

'Ahhhhh!' she screamed again.

'Shush,' said Dave, 'it's a dox, this is his master. This dox has just saved this man's life. He deserves a medal for what he done, not you screamin' ya lungs out.'

'What's a dox?' A small voice asked from the other side of the darkened room.

'Now look what you've done,' the nurse blustered. 'You've woken the leukaemia patient with all your noise.'

'I haven't made any noise at all, madam, so

shush and the little boy can get back to sleep.'

'I'm a girl,' the voice said. 'My name's Maria and I want to know what a dox is.'

Dave was trapped in a conversation, something he'd been avoiding for decades. He was also upset by the fact that he'd carried his only friend for eleven kilometres and then ridden with him over the range to the only hospital in the district and all the nurse wanted to do was scream.

'See,' Nurse Foran snapped, 'this little girl is very sick and you've burst into her room and dumped this man and his … vermin in her room.'

'Sorry, miss,' Dave addressed Maria, 'my mate's had a bad accident in the bush and I've carried him on me back for ages and then the horses …'

'But you can't just dump him where you like, this patient needs all the …'

'I'm not a patient. I'm Maria and I want to know what that animal is. It looks like a fox with a collar.'

Albert moaned and at last the nurse's professional instinct took over and she took his wrist to feel his pulse.

'Well, miss …' Dave began.

'Maria.'

'Maria. Well, it's not really a fox, it's like a cross between a fox and a dog. It's a dox.'

'Rubbish,' Nurse Foran blurted as she examined Albert's arm, 'no such thing.'

'Why's he got a ruby on his collar?' Maria asked, noticing the dull gleam of the gemstone winking in the light from the corridor.

'Because … because he's a really special dox and he belongs to me mate.' Dave turned to Albert. 'This poor fella here with the broken arm.'

'Who said it's broken? I've seen worse,' the nurse said firmly, her voice belying the gentleness with which she cut Albert's shirt away from his arm and removed his boots.

Ever smelt a bushman's socks? Nurse Foran had smelt a few in her time and Albert's weren't the worst by any means, and so she calmed a little and began organising splints and drips, beds and bandages in a blur of efficiency. Part of her bluster came from the fact that Doctor Glock was a stickler for pristine sheets and polished floors and had a way of making Nurse Foran feel like dirt beneath his feet if he found even the slightest blemish in *his* hospital.

'So,' Maria pursued her questioning, 'how did your friend get a dox?'

'Well, Albert is a really kind man you see ...'

'Albert? Albert you say?' Nurse Foran looked closer at the patient she was covering in snow-white sheets, 'Albert Cutts? Is this Albert Cutts?'

'Yes,' Dave replied.

'Why didn't you say so, you stupid man?'

'You wouldn't stop screaming.'

Nurse Foran ignored Dave's pertinent comment. 'Albert Cutts is a good man. Everyone says so.'

'And you must be Crazy Dave,' Maria said, 'my dad's told me about you.'

Dave slumped into a chair and watched as the nurse bathed and dressed Albert's arm. It always turned out like this. Every time he came into town it was always, 'Ah, look there's Crazy Dave.'

'You don't look crazy to me,' Maria said.

'Neither's Albert,' Nurse Foran added. 'There are some men who never hurt a fly. Not many mind you, but Albert's one of them. My sister would have married him if he'd ever asked.'

Dave said nothing. Albert was well known for his kindness and honesty. He was considered a bit of a curiosity for the lonely life he led, but he was respected. No one called Albert crazy.

'Are you crazy?' Maria insisted.

'He's different that's all,' the nurse interrupted. As she injected painkiller into Albert's … well, bum. Where else would you administer a painkiller? 'Some men just keep to themselves and get on with their lives in private. That's the way Albert has always lived. The man who woke you up with all his noise may be the same. Probably a respectable man if the truth is known, even if he does drag vermin into a little girl's ward.' Nurse Foran ignored the fact that Fog and Queenie had slipped under the bed and out of sight.

'Do you like being called Crazy?' Maria asked.

Dave didn't answer.

'They call me Constipation,' Maria continued, 'Because my name's Coniliopoulos. They think it's funny.'

'Some people are easily amused,' Nurse Foran

assured Maria, 'especially kids at school.'

Nurse Foran should know. Her mother must have had a brain seizure the day her daughter was born and called her Nora. Nora Foran. Borin' Foran, Gnawin' Four an' Twenty pies. Borin' Nora Foran Twenty. Funny as a dead pigeon, the kids at Nora's school. 'Ahh,' the boys would pretend to vomit, 'this pie's disgustin', it's Borin' Nora Foran Twenty.' Hah, hah, very funny.

'People will say anything sometimes to hurt other people. Don't worry too much about it Maria. I'm sure David doesn't. Especially with a good friend like Albert. Who'll live to one hundred if I'm any judge.'

'How's his arm?' Dave risked a question.

'The arm is good, but some of the fingers could be better. Just as well you brought him when you did. Accidents like this can cause toxic shock. You've saved his life, David.'

'Fog done it, nurse, Fog saved his life. Fog come and got me. Without Fog Albert would still be trapped by the log. Fog is the real lifesaver, nurse.'

'Nora, David, I think you can call me Nora.'

'Nora Foran?' Maria asked, suddenly realising why Nurse Foran knew so much about how names can hurt.

'Yes, Maria, Nora Foran. Now I suggest you get some sleep so that you don't wake up the new patient, and you David … ah …'

'McKinley.'

'Mr McKinley, I suggest you take these animals home and come back in the afternoon when Albert will be in a much better condition.'

Maria watched the dox and dog follow Dave out of the ward.

That's not a dox, she said to herself, that's just a fox with a collar. But I still don't know *why* it's a fox with a collar.

»→*«←

Dave came back later in the day but Albert was asleep. They couldn't shift him easily while he was so ill so he was still in Maria's room.

Dave didn't know what to do so he sat in a chair and pretended to read a magazine about film stars and princesses.

'Where's the dox?' Maria asked from behind him.

Dave had hoped she'd be asleep too.

'At Albert's house. I took him back there to keep Brim company.'

'You both live in the bush?'

'Yes.'

'Do you get lonely?'

'No, I've got a dog.'

'What's its name?'

'Bess.'

'Bess, that's a short name.'

'Queenie Bess.'

'Queenie Bess. That's better. I like that. What sort of dog is she?'

'You saw her last night, she's part dingo.'

'You really are strange aren't you? A fox and a dingo.'

'Fog is a dox, I told you that.'

'I think it's a fox with a collar.'

Dave shrugged.

'I read all day and watch Discovery Channel every chance I get. What else is there to do in here? I know a lot about animals.'

'You like animals?'

'Of course, doesn't everyone?'

'Some don't. It's good that you can learn about them while you're in here.'

'I'm dying.'

It was like a sledgehammer hitting a wedge. The two blows rang as clear in the room as struck metal in a frosty valley. Dave's ears hummed in surprise and confusion.

'I heard them tell Mum. They thought I was asleep. I knew I could trick them into telling the truth.'

'I'm sure … ah …' Dave knew that as the only conscious adult in the room it was his job to reassure the child that she'd be fine. 'I'm sure … ah … I'm sure the doctors have …'

'No, I'm dying. They said so. Mum cried all over the place. She's still crying. Every time she comes in that's all she does.'

Dave stared at her, meeting her eyes for the first time, entranced by the overwhelming hopelessness of any dumb lie he could think up. He kept his mouth shut.

'You know what I'd like to do?' she said.

'No,' he answered with relief. It was any easy question to answer. He had no idea what dying children wanted to do. Apart from live.

'I'd like to see your dox. I'd like to pat her.'

'It's a him. Fog. He's a boy. It's Albert's fox really.'

'There, you said it. Fox.'

Dave stared stupidly, not crazily, but dumb, nothing smart to say.

'You admitted it was a fox. You're scared people will shoot it if you say it's a fox aren't you?'

Dave swallowed hard but his head nodded in ascent.

'I think it'd be wonderful to have a wild animal as a friend. That's why I want to see where you live. You and Albert.'

'But there's no road, just a track, you'd … '

'You carried him on the track. You told Nurse Foran. Nora Foran.'

'Yes, but it's an awful long way and … '

'But you carried him and he's big. I'm little, skin

and bone, they say.'

'But … '

'I'll ask my mum. She'll let me. She doesn't know what else to do.'

THE RIVER

It was a strange sort of parade: the narrow track beneath the flowering wattles and geebungs; the dox and dogs trotting beside them; Albert with his arm in a sling; Dave carrying Maria on his back; and Mrs Coniliopoulos crying at the rear.

They arrived at Albert's house and Dave bustled about putting a plank between two stumps so that everyone could sit down. Albert only had two chairs.

The billy was on and the two men, not used to

having visitors, awkwardly offered tea.

Dave remembered Maria and tested all his knowledge of the beverage preferences of ten-year-old girls.

'I'm sorry, Maria, there's no lemonade.'

'That's all right,' she said, 'I want tea anyway, out of that billy.'

'There's no milk either,' Albert added.

'Black tea, I want black bush tea, like you.'

So they all sat around drinking black tea and eating a box of cakes Nora Foran had given them, leftovers from yesterday's hospital meals.

A bird skittered at their feet.

'What's that?' Maria asked.

'It's a scrub wren,' Albert replied, 'a white-browed scrub wren. He's really friendly. Comes into the hut to eat the crumbs. He's actually a girl.'

'How do you know that?' Maria sounded sceptical. She thought *she* was the one who knew everything about animals.

'It's got a grey face, the boys are darker, almost black. She's probably feeding babies. Crumble up some cake and drop it, she'd love that.'

The little bird skipped about Maria's feet until a yellow robin flitted into the clearing, clipped its feet onto the side of a wattle tree and glared at the scrub wren. Any cake being given out was his cake too. But really the robin wasn't so keen on cake. He only turned up to see if Albert was splitting firewood or turning over his vegetable garden. Both those jobs produced grubs and the robin loved grubs. The fatter the better.

Maria asked about each of the birds that visited: the comical family of choughs that she'd seen out her window, and now here they were again, metres from her chair and she could hear the little mewing, that conversation of happy families. She couldn't believe how beautiful the king parrots were when you could see them close up. And the whip bird. The currawong that called out barricello all day. The red-browed firetail, which Albert called towerer in his grandfather's language. He told her that he thought the firetail's red beak was like a piece of red enamel, like nail polish. Maria loved them all, never having been so close to wild birds before.

She was amazed that they weren't scared of Fog or Brim or Queenie Bess. Especially Fog, a fox, an animal designed to kill birds. But Fog sat on Maria's lap and let himself be patted until the coat around his neck shone like gold. He licked her face in appreciation and she shrieked with delight.

Her mother just shrieked. 'That fox will make her sick!'

'I love it here,' Maria declared, 'with all my friends.'

Mrs Coniliopoulos burst into tears again. Dave turned to her and was about to say shush but remembered his manners in time. It was just that Dave hated too much noise.

'Tell you what,' said Albert, 'what about we go fishing next week when my arm's a bit better? We can use Tiger's boat.'

'The doctor said … ' Mrs Coniliopoulos began.

'Mum, let me go, *please*. I'm sick of being stuck in that room.'

'But you might get tired and … '

'Well, I'll go to sleep. Please, Mum, I've never been fishing.'

She wasn't a naughty or persistent girl and she didn't usually argue much with her mother but she loved the forest and now the thought of the river was too much. Mrs Coniliopoulos really would do anything for her daughter as long as it was for the best. But how did you know what was best when she was so ill?

Albert gently convinced Mrs Coniliopoulos that they could make the day not too strenuous and Maria could always rest at Tiger's if she needed to. Somehow Albert managed to mention Tiger's horses. Maria had heard of the heroic performance of those beasts and her eyes shone with such expectation that Mrs Conillipoulos' misgivings crumbled in the face of her daughter's enthusiasm.

Maria was a town girl. For the last eight months she had been locked up with nature shows and books, which had filled her with enormous volumes of information but no experience. She wanted to touch the animals, spy out the wild beasts, catch the elusive fish and smell the wild, wild wilderness of Tiger's river.

»→ ＊ ←«

Maria couldn't believe Tiger's farm; there were kids and animals everywhere. The kids seemed to compete in offering Maria different fruits and cakes form Lily Carter's kitchen. She accepted all the gifts but couldn't face eating them. All the medication she was on had stolen her appetite.

'What's wrong with ya, anyway?' Possum Carter, the second youngest, demanded. 'Dad says yer real crook.'

'I've got leukaemia.'

'Are ya gunna die?'

'Shh, you, Possum,' his older sister Alice scolded.

'Maria is on a new medication and the doctor's are very hopeful there will be an improvement,' Mrs Coniliopoulos intervened.

The look Maria gave Possum and Alice left them feeling that Maria didn't share her mother's confidence, if, indeed, that's what her mother believed.

'They said I was too sick to go out in the bush, but I've never been fishing and Albert promised.'

'Here's some scrubbies for ya then,' Possum declared.

Maria looked sceptically at the yoghurt container full of squirming worms.

'They're scrub worms, terrific bait for perch and bass.'

Tiger came over leading three horses.

'Here are the three heroes you wanted to see, Maria, aren't they beauties?' He lifted Maria into the saddle of old Sparkle and his heart clenched with sorrow. The kid weighed almost nothing. 'I'd put you on the superhero, Fair Go, but he can be skittish at times. Behaved himself when it was important, but most of the time he still thinks he's racing in the Melbourne Cup.'

'Did he win the Melbourne Cup?' Maria gasped.

'In his dreams,' Tiger scoffed, 'old Fair Go here never won a race in his life. Led quite a few of them but then got a bit too interested in the fillies behind him. Had a bit of trouble that way meself.' Tiger winked at his wife, who blushed and dug him in the ribs.

'Horses don't dream, do they?' Maria questioned. She could be a bit of a know-all sometimes, but when you know a lot it's sometimes hard not to show it off.

'I think Fair Go dreams, Maria. When he took charge of getting Albert to hospital he dreamt he was a good, reliable horse. Mind you, he's woken up since. Ate an entire crop of peas yesterday and then came sookin' to me because he had a bellyache. But he's got brownie points now, reckons he can get away with anything.'

Albert and Dave weren't going to get far without a cup of tea so they sat around a big wooden table under the peppercorn tree. Tiger had found the table at the tip and patched it up. Lily brought out a batch of scones and johnnycakes and Tiger declared that all the ingredients were produced on the farm.

'What about the flour, Dad?' Alice asked.

'And the salt?' Possum questioned through an entire scone with jam and cream so that his words sounded like 'Vodda boud va thol?' No-one understood him so no-one replied. They were used to Possum.

'Yeah, Dad, and the tea leaves in the tea?' Col asked and winked at Maria, who realised there were others at the table who liked to air their knowledge.

'Look, you mob,' Tiger began, clearly thinking on his feet to combat the sharp questioning of his children, 'I'm not talking about condiments. Condiments aren't food. They're … like … like extras to the food. I'm talking about the milk an' butter, the jam an' honey an' almonds an' stuff, the things we grow here.'

'Pass the condiments, will you, please, Mum?' Colin asked and everyone laughed at his cheek, even Tiger. Dave laughed too despite the fact that he'd had the sharper edge of Colin's tongue before.

Colin was awkward in front of Dave for the same reason and took the opportunity, while the rest of the company continued analysing the ingredients of every item on the table, to speak to Dave for the first time that day.

'Dad said you carried Uncle Albert all the way from the mountain.'

'Yes,' Dave replied without meeting the boy's eyes. He'd already told him this before but this was Colin's awkward way of apologising.

'That's a lot of Ks to carry someone.'

'It's just a walking track. Can't get a car in there. There was no time to wait around … and … he's me mate.'

Mate, thought Colin, a mate of me uncle's, mate enough to carry ninety kilograms eleven kilometres in the dark. That's a decent sort of mate.

'Come on, you lot,' Tiger declared, glad to be free of his interrogation. 'We've gotta get Maria down to the river to catch some fish.'

Maria was lifted on to Sparkle again and Dave held the reins to reassure Mrs Coniliopoulos. They couldn't trust the hero Fair Go, not after a bellyful of peas.

Down by the river Albert showed Maria how to thread worms on a hook and how to cast from the hand reel. Fog sat beside Maria but his restless eyes roved about the riverbank and the camp that Dave had set up to make Mrs Coniliopoulos comfortable.

Brim leant against Albert after he sat down beside Maria and became as absorbed as the humans were by the slow, intricate life of the river: the parrots and pardalotes in the trees; the dragonflies shimmering above the water; and the rainbow birds dashing across the river in their blaze of colour.

Maria had read about them before, all of them, but seeing them was different. Seeing how they behaved told her more about the nature of birds and animals than seeing them in brilliant full colour on a page. Albert told her about each of the birds and had a story, often several, to indicate what moved the bird's soul. Albert didn't use the word soul. He'd say things like: 'Now this little fella, watch how carefully it looks after the younguns.' 'See that swan there, always puts herself between us and the cygnets, giddi, we call the babies.'

He told her of the stingless bush bee that was being pushed out of its country by the European bees with their relentless search for new territory. Albert had the knowledge and experience to complement her encyclopedic collection of facts.

Maria pointed out an old kangaroo resting under the shade of a river gum and Albert explained how thin he was, his ribs and breastbone showing through his hide.

'That ol' fella, see, he's been king of the mob in his day but one of the young bucks took him on and now this poor ol' man is kicked out, on his own. Oh he'll mooch along like this for a year or two an' then one frosty morning we'll find him dead.' And Albert would have choked off that last word if he'd been quick enough.

'Like Brim,' Maria said, 'when she gets really old.'

'No, no, not like Brim, she'll always have a mate to the end. She's not gunna die cold and alone.' Gees, I'm thick as a brick, I've gone and used the D word again.

When Brim heard her name she squirmed into Albert's side, looking up at him in adoration, showing the tip of her tongue between her lips. Fog wasn't going to be outdone and reached down and licked Maria's hand twice in little dabbing foxy licks. Doxes weren't demonstrative like dogs, they were wild creatures and set themselves slightly apart. Even Fog, with all his loyalty, spent most of his time avoiding the gaze of people and staring over the river with an aloof stillness. He'd glance back at Albert every minute or so to check on him and had chosen to sit beside Maria because he sensed that's what Albert wanted. But for all that, he was a dox not a dog.

'What will happen to Fog?' Maria asked, stroking the dox between the ears, smoothing the golden fur.

'Oh, he'll be all right,' Albert replied, desperately trying to construct a sentence without the D word in it. 'He'll always have a mate.'

'Yes, but what if he wants a real mate, like a girl fox?'

'Well, that's up to him.'

'But he's your pet.'

'No, Fog is a fox, Maria. We call him a dox so that people won't kill him, but he's a fox and one day he'll go.'

'But you love him and he loves you … He saved your life.'

'Yes, and I saved his. Under normal circumstances he'd be … He'd never have survived after his mother … got taken. But who's to say I did the right thing? He's a feral animal, he's not supposed to be here.'

'So why did you?'

'Because I couldn't help myself. You should have seen him when he was a cub. Him and his sisters.'

'Sisters?'

'Oh, yes, he had two sisters and after they grew up they went back to being foxes, eating baby birds and trying to kill chickens … That's what foxes do.'

'So Fog will go one day?'

'Don't know. We've never spoken about it. You ask him.'

Maria turned the dox's head so that she could look into his eyes.

'Is that what you'll do, Fog, leave all your friends?'

Fog's eyes were inscrutable. As inscrutable as a fox.

Brim squirmed closer between Albert and Maria and licked the girl's hand as if to say, I'll stay, I'll stay, I'm not a stuck-up fox.

'I love them both,' she said, 'I'd hate to think of one of them not being with you.'

'Well, that's the way it is. If it happens, it happens.'

'Like me,' she said and tried to catch his eye. But suddenly Albert got busy with the lines.

'Thought that was a bite for a minute,' he said before settling again, thinking he'd avoided the question. If it was a question.

'I might die.'

'Yes, you told us, first day in the hospital. But you're on a new treatment now, the doctors said ...'

'It might work.'

'Yes, and Fog might stay, and might is better than won't.'

Maria thought about it.

It was unnerving talking to her because she was so intelligent and the threat of her illness, the possibility that she might die, had focused her mind to pinpoint concentration on the fundamentals. Of life. The nature of being alive. She didn't speak as a child her age would speak.

And yet she was thrilled with the things a child would be thrilled by: the beauty of birds and animals, the hectic glory of the country. To be thrilled was to be alive. And she was thrilled.

Albert was saved from further questioning by catching two lovely perch and a blackfish. Tiger put them in the coals of the fire and told Colin to take Dave and Maria to get some yabbies.

Colin rowed them in silence across the river while the rainbow birds stitched threads of vibrant colour about them.

'Look,' Colin said at last. 'Look, there's Bunjil looking out for us.'

Maria looked where he pointed and there was a wedge-tailed eagle weaving great lazy circles in the sky.

'That's our spirit bird. When we see him everything's all right.'

Everything? Maria thought to herself, but couldn't help admiring the huge bird wheeling giant circles around the sun.

On the other side of the river they pulled in the yabby pots and tipped the catch into a bucket. Fog peered into the bucket with obvious distaste for such spiky, clawy, scratchy looking things.

But they tasted terrific. Tiger tipped them into

a kerosene tin of boiling water and soon they were eating a meal of fish and yabbies and fresh damper while the orioles and shrike thrushes called about them.

The shrike thrush entered the camp, his head tipped to one side enquiringly while keeping an eye on the dogs and fox.

Albert tipped the bird some crumbs of damper.

'Yarren, we call that one. He's a good bird. Lovely to have one around the camp. He's a good friend of our people. He'll sing for us later. He's got a beautiful voice.'

They drank more tea and dozed in the sun, mesmerised by the fragrant smoke from the red gum wood, deeply satisfied by the food they'd eaten. Queenie Bess was already asleep with her head on Dave's boot while Fog and Brim were like bookends beside the frail little girl.

'I'm going to remember this forever,' Maria declared.

And she did.

The author
Bruce Pascoe is a writer who can't go to sleep
without patting his dogs first. When he wakes up in
the morning the first thing he does is walk with his
dogs as they investigate the dawn. Bruce has written
26 books, lives at Gipsy Point, Victoria, on the
magnificent Genoa (Jinoor) River. He lives with his
wife, Lyn, has two children, two grandchildren and
two dogs, Yambulla and Wangarabel, named after
the mountain and town near where they were born.
Bruce's previous two dogs, Brim the dingo dog and
Reg the Independent are now sleeping in sunshine
a long way from earth. Bruce has a Bunurong-
Tasmanian heritage and the job he enjoyed most
was being dog wrangler for the vet at Maningrida,
Northern Territory.